CITY FUN

A Follett JUST Beginning-To-Read Book

CITY FUN

Margaret Hillert

Illustrated by Barbara Corey

FOLLETT PUBLISHING COMPANY
Chicago

Library of Congress Cataloging in Publication Data

Hillert, Margaret.
  City fun.

  (Follett just beginning-to-read books)
  SUMMARY: As two girls explore the city, they
watch buildings being torn down and built, ride
the subway, visit the park, watch a parade, play
games, and visit the library.
  [1. City and town life—Fiction] I. Corey,
Barbara. II. Title.
PZ7.H558Ci   [E]   80–14564
ISBN 0–695–41457–7 (lib. bdg.)
ISBN 0–695–31457–2 (pbk.)

Library of Congress Catalog Card Number: 80–14564

International Standard Book Number: 0–695–41457–7 Library binding
                                            0–695–31457–2 Paper binding

First Printing

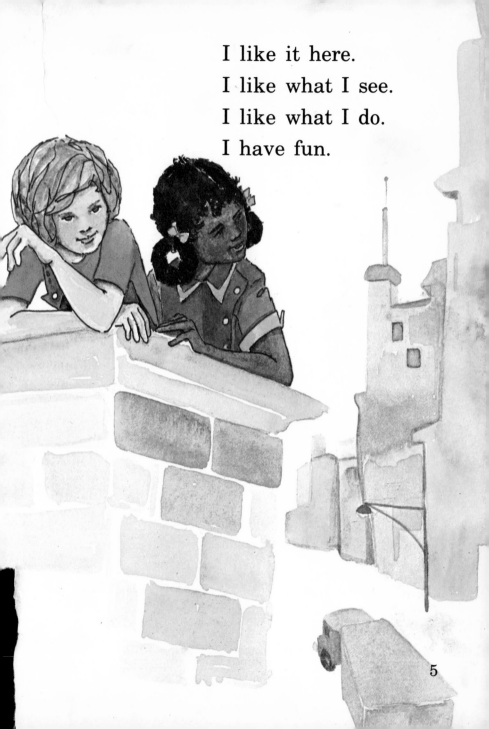

I like it here.
I like what I see.
I like what I do.
I have fun.

5

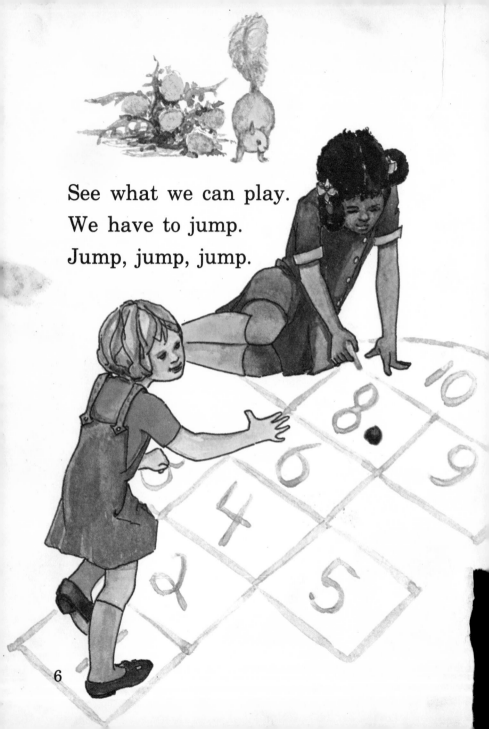

See what we can play.
We have to jump.
Jump, jump, jump.

6

And we can do this.
Look at us go.
We have to work at this.

Here is something
to look at.
See it go up.
Up, up, up.

And look at this.
It will come down.
Down, down, down.

Away, away, away.
We will ride away.
What a good ride.

I see something.

Red ones, yellow ones, blue ones.

I will get one.

Here is one for me.

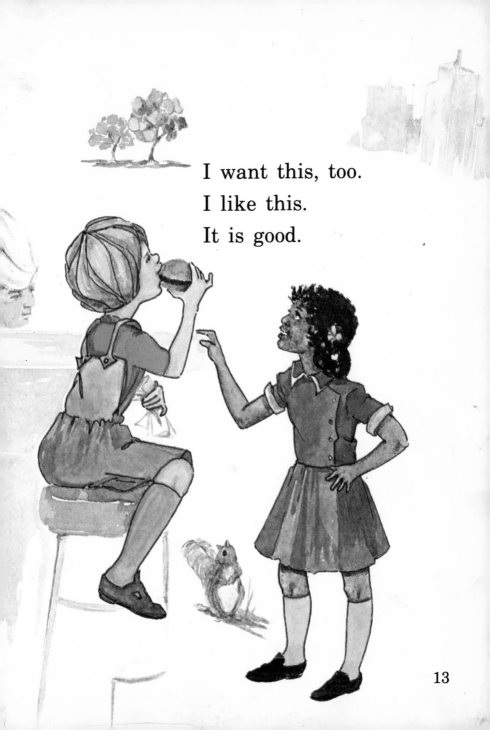

I want this, too.
I like this.
It is good.

13

Now see what we can do.
It is fun to do this.
Look out. Look out.

Oh, look at that.
Here it comes.
What fun. What fun.

Look at this.
See what I can do.
I like it.
I like it.

It is fun up here.
Way, way up here.
And I like to look down.

I like to see the boats.
Big boats.
Little boats.
Go, boats, go.

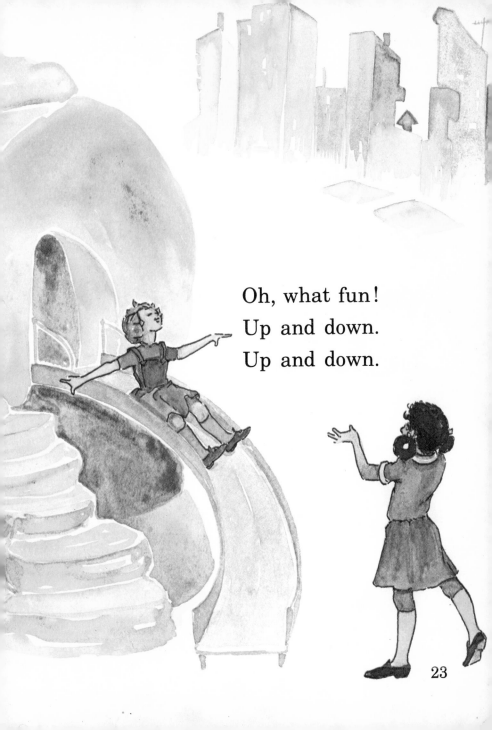

Oh, what fun!
Up and down.
Up and down.

23

We can go up and down, too.
We can jump, jump, jump.
1 and 2 and 3 and 4 . . .

Here is a man.
What will he do?
What can he do for us?

Oh, oh, oh.
Look at this.
Come in. Come in.
It is good in here.

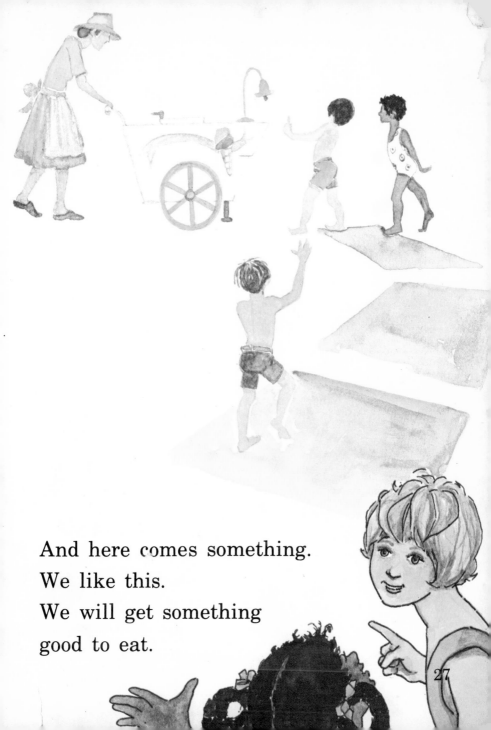

And here comes something.
We like this.
We will get something
good to eat.

27

Come here. Come here.
Guess what we can do in here.
Guess. Guess.

We can get something.
You will like it.
You can take it with you.

I like it out here.
It is fun to sit here.
It is fun to do
what we do.

Margaret Hillert, author of many Follett JUST Beginning-To-Read Books, has been a first-grade teacher in Royal Oak, Michigan, since 1948.

City Fun uses the 58 words listed below.

a	get	man	take
and	go	me	that
at	good		the
away	guess	now	this
			to
big	have	oh	too
blue	he	one(s)	
boats	here	out	up
			us
can	I	play	
come(s)	in		want
	is	red	way
do	it	ride	we
down			what
	jump	see	will
eat		sit	with
	like	something	work
for	little		
fun	look		yellow
			you